Shark Party

by DAVY OCEAN

Illustrated by Aaron Blecha

templar

Book Six:

Shark Party

With thanks to Paul Ebbs

A TEMPLAR BOOK

First published in the UK in 2014 by Templar Publishing,
an imprint of The Templar Company Limited,
Deepdene Lodge, Deepdene Avenue,
Dorking, Surrey, RH5 4AT, UK
www.templarco.uk

Text and concept copyright © 2014 by Hothouse Fiction
Illustration copyright © 2014 by Aaron Blecha

www.harry-hammer.co.uk

First edition

ISBN 978-1-84877-926-6

Printed and bound by CPI Group (UK) Ltd,
Croydon, CRO 4YY

Chapter 1

"Muuuuuuuuuuuuuuuuuuuuuuuuuuum!
Stop it! It's breakfast time. I want to
eat my breakfast. I want to enjoy my
breakfast. I don't want to talk about
exams! I want to concentrate on
breakfast. Are you trying to give me
findigestion before I even start eating?"

I don't think Mum is listening. She's swimming around the kitchen, preparing breakfast on auto-pilot – slooooooooooooow auto-pilot. There are kelp krispies popping and crackling in a bowl as they go soft (and kelp krispies are rubbish when they're mushy). And she hasn't even put the crab pop-tarts in the toaster yet! All she's interested in doing is going on and on about the Quay Stage 2 exams I've got to take next month at school.

"Well, Harry, I know revising isn't your favourite pastime," Mum says for the third time, as she swims right past the pop-tarts, "but it really is important..."

In my head I'm yawning. It's a BIG yawn. Not as big as the hungry hole in my tummy, but it's close.

Dad is no help at all. He's got his hammerhead stuck in today's Seaweed Times, scanning the pages to see if there's anything about him. Dad's Mayor of Shark Point, and usually there's a picture of him in the paper opening a new building, or kissing a new-spawn, or standing next to an important visitor from another reef.

He likes to cut the stories out and put them up on the wall of his office. Today, he doesn't seem to have found anything about himself. This always makes him grumpy.

"Dad," I say, "could you pass my kelp krispies, ple—?"

"Not one picture!" Dad slaps a fin against the paper. "I had a dozen photos taken yesterday and not a single one has made it into the paper. It's like I don't exist!" Dad does like to exaggerate when he gets upset. I've got to do something RIGHT NOW, so that:

1.   Mum stops talking about exams.

4

2.   Dad stops talking about himself.

3.   My breakfast moves from the counter to my mouth before the rumbling in my tummy causes a seaquake!

And then I see it.

As Dad grumpily holds up the newspaper, I see an advert for the new Fintendo SeaWii-DS on the back.

Oh WOW!

All the hunger is pushed from my tummy as I fin up close to the back page. Dad is still huffing and muttering behind it, but I don't care.

I'm too busy looking at the advert for the ultra-new fin-held games console, with SeaWii-D graphics, and Super Snapper Races 8. And it's out today.

I WANT ONE!!!!

"Now, about this revision..." Mum says, finally putting the crab-tarts in the toaster.

But I'm not listening, I'm reading all the mouth-watering specs in the advert:

1. SeaWii-D Screen!
2. Depth-Charge Slider!
3. Circle Pad Canalogue Control!

4.   WiFi-sh Communication!

5.   TONS OF OTHER GREAT THINGS THAT
      I DON'T REALLY UNDERSTAND BUT ARE
      PROBABLY THE BEST THINGS EVER IN
      THE FISHTORY OF THE SEAVERSE!!!

It all looks so cool.

"Mum!" I say, stabbing my fin so hard into the newspaper it goes right through and plonks Dad on the hammer. "Can I have one of these? Please, please? Pretty please with a side order of please?"

Dad looks at me angrily through the hole in the paper, and Mum catches the two crab-tarts as they pop out of the toaster. "No!" they both say at exactly the same time, like they've been practising.

"Why?" I ask, sawing around the advert with my fin so that I can stick it on my wall.

"Because they're bad for you," Mum says, finally bringing my breakfast over.

BAD FOR ME?!

I stare at her so hard my eyes nearly pop out of my hammer. What is wrong with her? How can something so good be bad?!

"You should be out playing with your friends, not stuck at home playing a silly computer game," Mum continues.

SILLY?! I'm starting to think Mum might actually have gone crazy.

"But, Mum, I'd have way more friends to play with if I had one of these. I'd be the most popular shark in Shark Point!"

But Mum just shakes her head. "There's no way I'm changing my mind, Harry. Anyway, you should be concentrating on your revision at the moment."

I can't believe she's being so mean! I'm her son. Her only son. Doesn't my happiness mean anything to her?

"I have rights, you know!" I say, puffing up my chest and sticking out my dorsal fin.

Mum looks at me like I've just broken her best vase with a finball.

"I do! I'll list them for you if you don't believe me."

Mum stares at me. "Go on, then."

"Oh, well, uh, number one: I have the right to – er – to develop proper fin-eye coordination!"

Mum just rolls her eyes.

"Number two: I – er – er – I have the right to express myself through getting the highest score at Super

Snapper Races 8!"

Mum starts tapping her fin on the counter.

"Number three: I have the right to new technology. I should not be left behind in the backwater of old stuff where all you old sharks live!" (I think I might be going too far, but I can't seem to stop now...)

TAP
TAP
TAP

"Number four: I have the right to have parents who love me enough to give me what I need to become a happy and healthy hammerhead shark!"

The kitchen is silent, except for a few pops and crackles as the last of my kelp krispies finally turn to mush. Mum is glaring so hard at me I turn to Dad.

"Tell her, Dad – I need a Fintendo, don't I?"

Dad peers over the top of the paper but he isn't looking at me, he's looking at Mum. "Harry, you definitely need something..." he says.

Yayyyyyyyyyyyy!

"You need to be grounded for a week and get no fin-money for a month if you don't apologise for upsetting your mum, right now!"

Oh.

Mum looks really angry. She snatches the advert from my fin, screws it up and throws it into the bin.

"Now you listen to me, Harry," she says. "If you don't get on with your revision and pass your exams, not only will you **not** be getting a Fintendo, but you won't be going to the end-of-term party either!"

Mum takes my breakfast (I hadn't

even started eating it!) and throws the bowl in the dishwasher. Then she crosses her fins and stares at me.

I don't believe it. No Fintendo. No breakfast. And the threat of no end-of-term party!

THIS IS SO UNFAIR.

I bang my hammer on the table. "I can't believe how mean you're being. You're lucky I don't report you to the National Society for the Prevention of Cruelty to Hammerheads!"

With that, I storm out of the kitchen and swim as fast as my tail will propel me to my bedroom.

I throw myself onto my bed and pound the seaweed blanket with my fins.

"What's up, Harry?" Humphrey, my humming-fish alarm clock, says. Larry the lantern fish (my bedside lamp) lights up and shines his glow on me.

"I am never, ever, ever, as long as I live, getting out of bed again," I wail, burrowing under the covers. "I am now the prisoner of the most evil dictator in the fishtory of shark kind."

"Who's that?" asks Lenny.

"MY MUM!!!!!!!!!" I shout from under the covers. "She doesn't care about my happiness. All she wants me to do is revise, revise, revise – and she knows how much I hate revision. She is so evil she makes the sting of sting rays feel like tickles, and the chomp of a great white feel like a kiss from your granny!"

"I think I'd rather be chomped by a great white," says Humphrey. "My granny smells like boiled sea-cabbage and has lips like a sea-cow's bum."

"Whatever!" I whine, sticking an eye out from under the cover. "My mum's evil, evil Mrs McEvil from Evilville-on-Sea!"

Just then, Mum swims into the room carrying my lunchbox and a tray. The tray contains a bowl of fresh kelp krispies and a plate of crab pop-tarts.

"I'm sorry I shouted at you, Harry, but you did make me very cross," Mum says. "Now make sure you have a big breakfast. You want to have plenty of energy for your schoolwork." She puts the tray down beside my bed and tucks my lunchbox into my school bag. "I've put an extra bag of krilled crisps in your lunchbox, so you don't go hungry during the day."

"Wow," Humphrey says as Mum swims out of the room. "That sounds like the most evil breakfast and lunchbox ever. What an evil dictator your mum is!"

Humphrey and Larry start to snigger behind their fins.

"It's just an act!" I shout. "She is evil! You didn't hear what she said to me in the kitchen." But Humphrey and

Larry are now floating on their backs surrounded by giggle-bubbles.

"Oi, Harry," says a voice at the window. I look up and see my best friends – Ralph the pilot fish, Joe the jellyfish and Tony the tiger shark – crowded at the windowsill. "Want a game of finball before school?" Ralph says with a grin. Tony heads a ball towards Joe, who clutches it in twelve of his legs, then uses a gusty bottom-pop to aim it at my bedroom window. I dive out of bed and flick it away with my tail.

Saved!

I grab my school bag and a finful of

crab pop-tarts and head for the window.

"I thought you were never getting out of bed again!" Humphrey calls after me. He and Lenny start laughing their heads off again as I swim away.

By the time I get to the park, I've calmed down a bit. We're just about to start the fin-about when we hear a crowd approaching.

"Wow!"

"WOW!!"

"WOW WOW WOW!!!"

"WOW!!! WOW!!! WOW!!! WOW!!!"

A stream of our school mates come through the park gates, flapping their fins in excitement.

"What's going on?" Tony says, swimming above us to get a better look. I push up to join him. They're all crowded round the broad back of a young bull shark.

"It's Billy," says Ralph, swimming up with Joe. "What's he holding?"

The other kids are all looking at something Billy has in his fins. I turn on my hammer-vision and use it to zoom in on the centre of the crowd.

My stomach flips.

Billy is holding a new Fintendo SeaWii-DS! He's playing Super Snapper Races like a pro. His fins are blurring across the controls and his eyes are fixed on the screen. I click off my hammer-vision and kick down towards him. I have to get a closer look at the console. Billy must have the best parents ever if they've bought him a Fintendo on the day it comes out!

Ralph and the others follow me as I shoulder my way through the crowd.

When I finally catch a glimpse of it my eyes goggle. It's as shiny as a black sea crystal and buzzing with noise and colour. It looks even better in real life than it does in the advert. Billy finishes the level he's on and hits a new high score.

The crowd goes wild!

I push up to him. "Billy, your Fintendo's awesome! Can I have a go?"

Billy looks up from the console and glares at me. "No way! I'm not lending this to anyone." He swims off towards the park gates.

The crowd moves on, following Billy like he's the coolest thing in the whole ocean.

It's so unfair! How come Billy gets a Fintendo and I don't? It's official – I have the evilest mum in the ocean!

Chapter 2

I don't feel any better by the time school starts, and my mood is not helped by our turtle-teacher, Mrs Shelby. She keeps droning on and on about revision for our exams. It's like being at home with Mum!

How do they expect me to think about exams now I've actually seen a new

Fintendo? I stare out of the window at the Year Three girls playing flounders. I'm not really that interested in flounders, but it's certainly more interesting than Mrs Shelby's fishtory revision.

"Harry!"

I jump as Mrs Shelby yells at me.
"Yes, Miss?"

"Do you think you can tell me about
King Moby the Eighth's first wife, Harry?"

"His first wife was called Harry?"
I say without thinking. My cheeks start
to go red as I realise the stupid mistake
I've made.

"No, Harry," Mrs Shelby continues
crossly. "Can you tell me her actual
name?"

Ralph, who's at the desk next to me,
whispers the answer into my ear. I turn
back to Mrs Shelby. "His first wife was
called Catherine of Plankton."

Mrs Shelby narrows her turtle eyes. "Correct. And what happened to her?"

I sneak a look at Ralph, who shrugs. I look across the room and see Joe, who pretends to scratch his head with some of his tentacles so Mrs Shelby can't see his face.

"I don't know," Joe mouths unhelpfully.

Great!

I can hear Rick Reef and his side-kick Donny Dogfish sniggering at me from the back of the room. My hammer is going pinker than a prawn burger.

Mrs Shelby sighs, and points back

to the interactive whitebait-board. "For the benefit of Harry – and anyone else who wasn't listening – Moby the Eighth was King of Fingland from 1509 to 1547. He had six wives – Catherine of Plankton, who he divorced, Anne Boatlyn who he had beheaded, Jane Seamour who died giving birth to Moby's only son Seaweed – who lived until he was just sixteen."

I bet King Moby wouldn't have put up with not having a Fintendo. He always seemed to get what he wanted.

"Then came Anne of Waves," Mrs Shelby continues, "who Moby divorced because he didn't like how she looked.

After Anne, Moby married Catherine
Sea-Coward, who hated Moby so much
that she had lots of other boyfriends – so
Moby had her beheaded too."

Moby is sounding pretty evil by
now – not as evil as my mum, but
getting there.

"Lastly, Moby married Catherine Starfish. Unfortunately, they also had no children, but stayed married until Moby died in 1547, leaving his only living child, Elobsterbeth, to become Queen."

I look around the class. It turns out that everyone else, even Rick and Donny, have been writing all of this down. I haven't written a word.

I've been too busy being annoyed at Mum and comparing her to Moby the Eighth. I lean over to Ralph to ask him if I can copy his notes later – but before I can say a word, the bell rings for break.

"**Wait, please!**" Mrs Shelby shouts as everyone starts getting up from their desks. "Before you go, I have an important announcement to make about the end-of-term party."

Everyone stops dead and listens. The end-of-term party is the best thing about school. Which makes Mum double-evil for threatening to not let me go. Mrs Shelby pushes her little round glasses up her flat turtle-face. "In fact, I have some very exciting news about the party."

We all stare at her, wide-eyed and open-mouthed. What could it be?

"This year," Mrs Shelby announces grandly, "there will be a competition to find the best dancer in the whole school!"

Is that it? I thought she said it was going to be EXCITING news. There's nothing exciting about dancing. All the boys start to groan. But the dolphin twins, Pearl and Cora, start swimming around with glee, high-finning and whooping. I don't know why they're so happy. Dancing is stupid and I can make a list to prove it. Dancing is stupid because:

1. Anyone doing it looks like they're desperate to go to the toilet.

2. The only kids interested in dancing are girls, and who wants to look like a girl?!

3. The only other underwater creatures who enjoy dancing are OLD PEOPLE who have nothing better to do on a Saturday night than watch Stickleback Come Dancing.

4. Seriously. Isn't that enough to put anyone off dancing FOR LIFE???

While I've been making my ultra-important list, Mrs Shelby has been making one of her own – listing all the reasons why dancing is great! Things like: it's really good exercise, it's a great way of making friends, and it's so much fun. I can hardly believe my ears. Is she crazy?!

"And finally," Mrs Shelby says, her voice all squeaky with excitement, "whoever comes first in the end-of-term dance contest will win a special prize!"

Hmmm, I wonder what that will be? A pink sparkly leotard and glittery fin warmers?

"The dancer with the best routine," Mrs Shelby says, "will win a brand-new

Fintendo SeaWii-DS!"

O.M.C.! (Oh. My. Cod.)

I'm so shocked, my hammer-head actually hits the desk. Mrs Shelby looks at me all worried.

I pick my face up and try and to make my mouth speak, but it's not easy. "W... wh... what did you say, Mrs Shelby?"

Mrs Shelby shakes her head. "Oh, Harry, I'm going to have to have a word with your parents. You haven't listened to a word I've said all lesson!"

"No – no – NO, Mrs Shelby. I was listening... I'm just not sure I heard that last bit right. Could you say it again?"

Mrs Shelby gives a big sigh. "I said that the student who does the best dance routine of the contest will win a brand new Fintendo SeaWii-DS."

"That's what I thought," I say and then everything becomes a big blur. All I can think about is the prize.

"Are you all right, Harry?" Tony says, as we swim out to the playground.

— An actual Fintendo!

"Open your mouth, Harry, I need a break-time snack," Ralph says.

A brand new Fintendo – for free!

I look around. Pearl and Cora have already taken over a corner of the playground and are busy practising their ballet moves.

"You sure you're all right, mate?" Ralph asks.

I nod. "Never better! Want to know why?"

Ralph's eyes widen hopefully. "Because you're going to let me snack on your leftover crab pop-tarts?"

I shake my head. "No. Because I'm

gonna win a Fintendo and it's going to be the easiest thing EVER!"

"You're going to dance?" Ralph laughs as I start flexing my fins and limbering up my hammer.

"You've always said dancing was stupid," says Joe. Purple flashes of confusion start running up and down his tentacles.

"Dancing is stupid," I say with a smile. "And that's exactly why I'm going to win!"

Joe's whole body starts flashing purple. "But..."

FLUBBBBBBERRRRRRRRR!!!!

Suddenly my head is shaking and the world looks like it's made from quivering rubber.

I hear Rick sniggering behind me. He's sneaked up and **boinged** my hammer. Ralph and Joe catch hold of each end of my head to try to stop it flubbering.

"You? Dance?" Rick sneers. "You couldn't dance your way out of a dead clam!"

"I-I-I... can... d-d-d-dance!" I stammer. My voice is all over the place – I sound like a Super Mario Carp backfiring on the starting-grid.

As my flubbering head slows down, Rick's pointy face comes into focus. He leans right into my hammer, his nose stuck between my eyes.

"That Fintendo is mine, Harry, and no stupid little stammerhead is going to get in my way!"

Chapter 3

I spend the rest of the day hardly able to concentrate on anything. When the final bell rings I zoom out of school, leaving Ralph and the others behind in a cloud of **WHOOSH!!!** I don't think I've ever got home so quickly.

I hardly notice the delicious smell of

freshly baked fishcakes coming from the kitchen. I fly up the stairs and hook my tail on the top banister to swing me round the coral corridor at insane speed.

"Harry, is that you? Do you want a fishc—?" is all I hear from Mum before I slam the door behind me, head for my desktop P-Sea and flick it on.

I need to surf the interwet, and I need to surf the interwet NOW.

Humphrey and Lenny float towards me and start looking over my shoulder.

"You still sulking, Harry?" Humphrey asks as the P-Sea boots up.

"Oh no! What's that smell?" Lenny

says, stifling a giggle. "Could it be your evil dictator mum making some deadly fishcakes? Shall we inform the authorities?"

"No, thank you," I tell them calmly.

"Are you logging on to the NSPCH website to tell them all about it?" Humphrey chortles.

The screen flickers to life. I do a quick search for the site I need...

"'The Life and Times of Moby the Eighth'?" Lenny reads. "Harry, what are you doing?"

"Revision, of course," I tell them.

"But you hate revision!" Lenny

exclaims, his light blinking.

"Not any more," I say.

"But..." says Humphrey.

"I don't understand..." says Lenny.

I sigh and turn to look at them. "If I don't revise, I won't pass my exams, and if I don't pass my exams, I can't go to the end-of-term party, and if I can't go to the end-of-term party, I won't be able to enter the dance competition, and if I can't enter the dance competition—"

"You won't turn into a girl?" says Humphrey.

"No," I say. "If I can't enter the dance competition, then I can't win the

dance competition, and if I can't win
the dance competition, I can't swim away
with a new Fintendo SeaWii-DS. And I
REALLY want a new Fintendo SeaWii-DS.
Now can you please be quiet? I have a ton
of catching up to do!"

I turn back to the screen and start
to read.

I wake up the next morning with my head on the P-Sea's keyboard and my chin covered in sleepy drool.

I must have fallen asleep revising.

I stretch my aching body and head downstairs. It's Saturday, so I'll have plenty of time for revision once I'm feeling a bit more awake. Dad comes swimming out of the kitchen with a finful of shrimp pop-tarts. I grab a couple for breakfast and look at Dad with my best hopeful goggly eyes.

Dad sighs and digs into his pocket.

He brings out buttons,
an old, rusty key,
some coral marbles
and (finally!) his wallet.

Saturday is fin-money day, and
I always spend it on a copy of 'Ready,
Steady, SHARK!' – my favourite sport
magazine. This week, I can't wait to get
it because they've got an interview with
the underwater-world-famous sharklete,
Turbo Tex.

"Are you all right, Harry?" Dad
says, as he hands me my money. "You
look really tired."

"Oh, I was just up late revising,"

I say casually.

Dad's eyes widen in surprise. "Really?"

I nod.

"Well, that's very good to hear. Very good indeed." He slaps me on the back. "Keep at it and one day you might even be as clever as me!"

"That would be cool, Dad!" I say with a grin.

After quickly eating my pop-tarts I head out into Shark Point. The water is still cool but I hardly notice. One half of my mind is on Turbo Tex, and the other is on the Fintendo I'm going to win at the end of term. Then suddenly I hear a girl's voice.

"No, you should do a tail twist with an over-kick."

I look around, and see Pearl and Cora on the opposite side of the street. They've got their bags over their shoulders and they're wearing sparkly pink fin-warmers. They're so deep in conversation they don't even notice me.

"Then I'll do a plié, followed by a pirouette," Cora says.

A WHAT followed by a WHAT?

"Ooh, yes," says Pearl. "That would be perfect! We are so going to win this dance competition!"

The girls high-fin and carry on down the street. So they were talking about dancing. Hmmm. This gives me an idea. Maybe they're going off to practise somewhere. I could spy on them and see if I can get a few tips for my own routine.

I drift over to the shadows at the edge of the street and start following them. I don't need to worry about being seen, though – they're way too busy talking about their routine.

I follow the twins all the way to a building on the outskirts of town. They swim up some rickety old stairs and disappear inside. I hear the faint sound of a piano playing. I've come too far to turn back now – if I'm going to learn a few dance moves from the girls, I'm going to have to look inside.

I creep up the stairs. As I reach the door at the top, the music gets louder, and I can hear the swishing of several tails. The door isn't completely shut, so I float up close to it and place a goggly eye by the gap. It takes a few seconds for my eye to adjust to the bright lights inside. The wall opposite me is covered with mirror-fish scales. A sign at the top of the wall reads:

MADAM L'OCTOPUS'S BALLET STUDIO

Ballet!

I'm not doing ballet in my dance routine – that's way too girly.

Pearl and Cora have joined a group of girl fish and dolphins. They're all dressed in pink ballet gear and they're warming up to the music.

There's nothing useful for me here. I start to swim away. But suddenly a thick, rubbery octopus tentacle shoots through the door and grabs me by the tail!

I'm hauled into the room with a **thud** and suddenly there's a huge greeny-pink face staring into mine. A high-pitched voice with a Trench accent screams in my ear.

"And what do we 'ave 'ere?"

"Harry!" Pearl yells.

"It's Harry Hammer, Madam L'Octopus," Cora says. "He goes to our school."

Madam L'Octopus stares at me. "And he is a ballet dancer, oui?"

"Well, I know he's good at dancing," Pearl says.

MADAM L'OCTOPUS'S BALLET STUDIO

I stare at her in shock.

Pearl grins back at me. "Because he's been telling everyone he's going to win the school dance competition."

"Veeery interesting," says Madam L'Octopus, waving me about in her huge tentacle. "Eet is about time we had a boy in this class. Let us see what the leetle dancey hammerhead can do."

The girls all giggle and start to clap along with the music. Madam L'Octopus lets go of me, but I can't escape. She's standing right between me and the door.

I'm trapped.

I can feel my face going pink. I

can't let Pearl and Cora see that I know nothing about dancing. They'll tell Rick and I'll be the laughing stock of the school – again!

I think back to what I overheard the twins talking about on the way here. What was it? Pliers? Piro-nets? I have no idea what those moves are, but I have to do something. So I start waving my tail in time to the music, and nodding my hammer backwards and forwards.

"I do believe 'ee can do ballet!" Madam L'Octopus cries, twirling around in a cloud of ink and rippling her tentacles with joy.

Hmmm, maybe this isn't going to be so difficult after all. Feeling a bit braver, I try to speed up. But then...

1. The girls form a circle around me, beating their fins in time.

2. I attempt a piro-net on my tail end (even though I don't actually know what that is) and clatter into a young hermit crab.

3. The hermit crab spins into Madam L'Octopus's mouth and causes her to have a coughing fit.

4. The coughing fit makes Madam L'Octopus squirt out a huge cloud of ink.

5. And suddenly no one can see where they are

or where they're going.

6. And I crash into about ten girls.

7. And I end up with my hammer covered in mirror fish scales, a pink fin-warmer on my dorsal, and someone's frilly ballet skirt on my head!

As the ink clears, Cora and Pearl swim right up in front of me with their Seaberry smart phones – and start taking pictures!

"Oh my cod! Everyone's gonna love this on Plaicebook!" Pearl shrieks.

Disaster!

"**You!**" Madam L'Octopus shrieks, pointing all of her twelve tentacles at me. "**You!!!**"

"Me, what?" I say, pulling the skirt off my head.

"You have ruined my mirror!"

We all turn to look at the far wall. The mirror-fish scales have all gone.

Everyone looks back at me. The mirror-fish scales are now covering my skin. Some of the girls start checking their reflection in me! I start hurriedly flicking the scales off with my tail.

"You have to pay!" Madam L'Octopus yells, wrapping one of her tentacles around me. "You must pay for zee damage!"

"But – but..." I stammer.

"But what?" she hisses.

"But I don't have any money," I reply. "Well, only my fin-money..."

"Zat will do!" she snaps.

I stare at her.

She glares back.

"Give eet to me, then!"

Pearl and Cora start fiddling with their phones, ready to take another picture of me. I quickly take my fin-money out of my pocket and give it to her.

"Now go!" Madam L'Octopus yells.

If she wasn't so scary I'd yell back, "Don't worry, I'm gone!" But she is scary – very scary – so I don't say a word and just swim for the door.

As soon as I get outside I bang my hammer against the wall in despair. It's so unfair! I didn't even want to go to a stupid ballet class. I only came out to get a copy of 'Ready, Steady, SHARK!' – and now I can't afford it!

I am totally fed up and completely broke. I brush the rest of the mirror-fish scales off me and start swimming home.

"Wow! You're so miserable you look like you've been given turtle toe-jam for lunch!" a girl's voice says as I turn the corner.

Brilliant. Another girl who wants to make fun of me.

Could today get any worse?

Chapter 4

I spin round, thinking it might be one of the girls from the ballet class. But it isn't.

A young leopard shark swims in front of me. She's wearing a cool Pike tracksuit. Her cap is on back to front and her neck is dripping with shipwreck bling.

"So, what's up?" she asks, giving

me a fin bump.
"Why you lookin' so
stressed? I'm Lola,
by the way. And
you're Harry
Hammer, innit?"

I look at her,
confused. "Yeah – er – how
do you know?"

Lola grins. "Seen you with your dad
in the newspapers."

"Oh." I'm not sure if she's about to
make fun of me so I don't smile back.

"It's all right. I don't bite," Lola
says. "Just saw you looking all grumpy

so I thought I'd see what the matter was. You don't have to tell me if you don't want to, though."

Lola's smile looks friendly, so I explain what happened back at the ballet school, and about the competition and the Fintendo prize.

Lola snorts with laughter, but it's not mean like Rick's – it's much more sympathetic.

"So you wanna learn to dance?"

I nod.

"Well, you ain't gonna learn how to win the competition at no ballet school. Ballet's well boring, innit?"

"I suppose."

"Proper dancing's learned on the street."

I frown. "What do you mean?"

Lola starts spinning on the spot, before doing a back flip and a star-fin. "See?" she says with a smile. "Want me to show you how?"

Suddenly I feel a million times better. "Yes, please!"

Lola nods. "Let's go to the skate park. I'll have you street dancing in no time!"

"Oh... I... I can't go there."

Lola puts her fins on her hips and

frowns at me. "Why not?"

"Well – er – my mum says I'm not allowed over there." I feel my face start to burn.

Lola shakes her head. "You some kind of mummy's shark? Maybe I should just take you back to ballet class, then!"

"No!" I yell. "I want to learn how to street dance and I don't care where I have to go to do it. I've got to win that Fintendo!"

Lola zooms past me, barrel-rolling into a skimming rush right past my hammer. Then she flicks out her fins and finishes with her tail bent up and her fins thrown back. It's the most brilliant dance move I've ever seen. "You sure you want to dance like this, Harry? It's not for mummy's sharks, you know!"

Right now I want nothing more than Lola to show me how to dance. She is one of the coolest sharks I have EVER met!

I nod again, this time totally sure.

"Come on, then!"

And **BANG!** She's off like a rocket.

We shoot down narrow alleys and through dark, dingy streets, heading towards South Central Shark Point. I've never been to this part of Shark Point before. The walls are covered in graffiti

and there are no houses, just coral blocks
and chain-link fences. We head past a
load of closed-down shops, and a row
of empty factories. The fish and sharks
around us seem bigger and scarier than
the ones I'm used to. I can hear police
sirens not too far away and whale trains

thunder overhead, dragging cargos of shipwreck metal.

Eventually, we come to the skate park. Behind rusty fences, the park is alive with sharks of all shapes and sizes. All of them are wearing Pike or FishHead sports gear. A gang of leopard sharks are riding yellow-finned skateboards.

"All right, Leon!" Lola calls to the nearest leopard shark. He looks round and jumps off his skateboard. Then he waves a fin to the others and, one by one, the gang coast to a halt, looking at me suspiciously.

Lola looks back at me. "Harry, this

71

is my dance crew – Shark Beatz." Lola
turns back to the gang. "Don't worry,
boys, this is Harry. He's cool."

Shark Beatz don't seem so sure,
though. Leon flicks his tail over, and
stares at me with narrow eyes. "He don't
look that cool to me, sis."

"I told you, he's all right." Lola
turns to me. "This is Leon.

He's my brother, and he's not as mean as he thinks he is."

Leon frowns, but doesn't say anything. He doesn't stop staring at me, though.

Lola beckons me forward with her fin. "Harry wants to learn how to dance. I brought him here so we could show him how to bust some moves."

Shark Beatz start to laugh out loud. Leon cracks a huge smile. "A hammerhead? Dance? Do me a favour, sis. All hammerheads are good for is knocking ships' nails into timber."

Lola nudges Leon. "Shut it, bruv. He needs our help, and we're going to give it to him, okay?"

I look at Lola. I'm not used to being stuck up for like this. It's making me feel a bit funny. I really hope it's not showing on my face. I stretch up to my full height. "Lola says you lot are the best dancers in all of Shark Point."

They nod.

"Well, I want to learn from the best."

This seems to do the trick, as the gang all put their skateboards to one side and form a circle around us.

Leon takes his phone from his pocket and starts playing a really cool ship-hop tune.

Lola starts flicking her tail back and forth to the beat. "Let's start with the most basic move – the Six Tail."

Lola and Leon go down on their bent tails, flicking them around in a circle and balancing their bodies on their fins behind them. They do six complete circles then stop and stare at me.

"Go, Hammer!" Leon calls.

I start to bend my tail, trip over it and smash my hammer in the stupidest self **FLUBBERRRRRRRRRRR** of all time.

Great.

My boinging head flubbers back and forth, and when it finally stops, Leon and the rest of Shark Beatz are floating on their backs holding their stomachs, laughing. I try the Six Tail again. This time, I bend, circle, fin-balance and **CRASH**.

FLUBBBBERRRR

Lola offers me a fin. "This might take longer than I thought," she says kindly as she pulls me back up.

Uver the next couple of hours, Shark Beatz show me how to do all of their best moves:

1. The Catfish Daddy (all loose fins and wobbly head).

2. The Treasure-Chest Pop (waves through the chest and a dorsal slap).

3. The Plop, Rock and Drop (a combination of a tail-plop, body-rock and falling over – I do the falling over bit REALLY well. I'm just rubbish at catching myself on my fins).

4. The Hammer-Dock (they made that one up

especially for me). And then, it's time for the hardest move of all...

5.   The Head Spin!

Lola turns herself upside down and with a flick of her fins, starts to rotate on her head. She gets faster and faster, as Leon and Shark Beatz cheer her on. She whirrs and blurs until I can't see her because she's moving so fast. Then **BANG!** She storms to a stop, fins out, tail flicked up to her dorsal, hanging there like the most radical and sick thing of all time.

We all start cheering. But almost immediately I feel gloomy.

How can I ever do anything as good as that?

"Your go, Hammer!" Lola calls as all of Shark Beatz swim up to her, finning her on the back.

"Okay!" I shout, and flip myself upside down.

I flick out with my fins. Because of my big, flubbery hammer, it takes a lot more work to get me moving than it does a sleek and beautiful leopard shark like Lola, but eventually, I start to spin.

The whole world starts to revolve as I flick and kick.

Kick and flick.

As I get faster, it's easier and easier to move through the water. The skate park becomes spinning streaks of colour...

I'm doing it.

I'm doing the hardest ship-hop move of all time.

The Head Spin!

I'm amazing!

I'm brilliant!

I'm a DANCER!

I'M A DANCER!!!

Even Shark Beatz are cheering me on. They're cheering and cheering and...

And... Actually... it doesn't sound

that much like cheering...

It sounds more like...

SCREAMING.

BOOOOOOOSH! I crash out of the
Head Spin and bounce onto the coral
floor with a painful crunch.

I look up dizzily.

Everyone is spinning around me as
if I'm still in the head spin. But I can feel
the rough coral against my back. It's NOT
ME who's spinning.

IT'S THEM!

Then I realise what's happened...

My stupid hammer is so big, I've
created an enormous whirlpool in the

middle of the skate park!

Everyone is tumbling head over tail around me like socks in a washing machine.

NOOOOOOOOOOOOOOOOOO!!!!!!!

Okay, I've messed up big time.

I'm on the wrong side of town, throwing a gang of tough sharks around like tadpoles in a sea tornado, and they are all screaming like girls.

I am going to be in trouble so big, a word has yet to be invented for how GIGANTI-HUGE it's going to be. I cover my hammer with my fins and wait for Shark Beatz to swim down and teach me a very painful lesson.

Except, something I'm not expecting to happen happens...

1.   The screaming in the whirlpool starts to change.

2.   The screams of fear become high-pitched

screams of laughter.

3. As the whirlpool caused by my hammer starts to slow down there's even more laughter.

4. I uncover my eyes and see Shark Beatz holding on to each other and laughing.

5. And as they all slow right down, and gain control of their fins and tails, they start cheering!

6. Cheering ME!!!!

"Ham-MER! Ham-MER!! HAM-MERRRRRRRRRRRR!!!!" they chant together. Leon has the widest smile on his face, and Lola swims down and hugs me tight in her fins!

This makes me go all goggly-eyed.

"Wow, Harry, that was amazing!" Lola says. "That was the greatest Head Spin we have ever seen. None of us have ever caused a whirlpool before!"

We all grab fins, touch tails and dance around like clown fish in a carnival – madly whooping, high-finning and generally laughing the teeth right out of our gums!

Even Leon comes over and shakes me by the fin. "Dude, I'm sorry I ever doubted you. You are gonna be a totally radical dancer. You're FINtastic!"

And I feel FINtastic!

Chapter 5

It's the first day of the exams and we're all waiting for Mrs Shelby to hand out our papers. At his desk across the room, Joe is turning a frightened shade of yellow. At the desk next to me, Ralph is trying to remember what happened to each of

Moby the Eighth's wives.

"Divorced, beheaded, divorced – no, died," he mutters. "Divorced – or was that one beheaded?" He looks at Tony. Tony is staring into space and flicking his tail nervously. Even Rick looks uneasy as he chews on his pencil fish. But for the first time ever, I don't feel too bad about having to take an exam. Over the past few weeks I've spent more time revising than I've spent eating

87

kelp krispies – and that's a lot! And when I haven't been revising, or eating kelp krispies, I've been learning how to dance at the skate park with Lola. Now I feel ready to take on anything!

"Make sure you take your time with your answers," Mrs Shelby says as she starts handing out the exams. "You don't want to make any silly mistakes."

I look down at the first question.

EXAM

What was King Moby's favourite sport?
a) Finball ☐
b) Flounders ☐
c) Hunting ☐

Hunting! I know because it came up when I was doing some last-minute revision this morning on my P-Sea.

I quickly tick the answer. Then I read the next question.

What was the name of King Moby's daughter?
a) Seaweedia ☐
b) Elobsterbeth ☐
c) Crabella ☐

Yes! I know that one too – I learned it when I got Humphrey and Larry to pretend to be Moby's children the other day. It was partly to help me with my revision and partly to get them back for teasing me about Mum not being evil.

I carefully tick the Elobsterbeth box with my pencil fish. Then I go on to the next question.

What did King Moby wear on his head?
a)   a starfish   ☐
b)   a jellyfish   ☐
c)   a crown fish   ☐

Crown fish! And so it goes on. Before I know it, I've finished the final question. I look around the classroom. The others are all still writing. I stare out of the window and start going through my dance routine in my head. Thanks to Lola's teaching, my Catfish Daddy is coming on really well. I start wobbling my head and waving my fins as I imagine myself at the dance contest. The other contestants are all cheering, the judges are clapping their fins in time, and I'm—

"Harry! What are you doing?"

I jump in shock. Mrs Shelby is floating at my desk, glaring at me.

"Why are you wobbling your head? Why aren't you doing your exam?" she asks crossly.

"I've finished, Miss."

Mrs Shelby sighs and shakes her head. "I told you not to rush, Harry. Rushing causes mistakes." She looks down at my paper. "Oh." She starts to smile as she reads through my answers. "Okay, well, just sit there quietly until the others have finished. No more head wobbling."

Head wobbling? Doesn't Mrs Shelby know a Catfish Daddy when she sees one?! But I can't help grinning. Who'd have thought that revising would make exams almost fun?

The week of the exams goes by faster than a rocket fish. I got a bit muddled up in Trench and got some of my sums wrong in maths, but mostly they went way better than normal. And the best thing is, Mum's so pleased with the way I revised she's said I can go to the end-of-term party no matter what I get. Result!!!

The day before the party I go to the skate park for one last practice. Lola and Leon are there waiting for me.

Lola's holding something for me in her fin.

"I got you this," she says, looking a bit embarrassed. "It's to bring you good luck at the dance contest, innit."

She swims closer to me. She's holding a thick anchor chain decorated in shipwreck bling. It's almost as big as Leon's.

"Cool! Thanks," I say as she goes to put it on me. Luckily it's big enough to fit over my hammerhead.

"And I got you something too," Leon says with a grin. He hands me a baseball cap. It's got Shark Beatz studded in coral on the front.

"Wow!"

"Now you're really one of the crew," Lola says, grinning.

"What, really?" I say, my eyes goggling in shock.

"Yeah, bruv," Leon says with a high fin. "You're our number one Head-Spinner."

"And you're gonna win that dance contest for sure!"

Lola does a quick back flip. "Come on, let's go and practise some Hammer-Docks."

Lola and Leon head off into the middle of the park. As I swim after them I feel like the happiest hammerhead alive. I've finished my exams and I'm allowed to go to the party. Now all I have to do is win the Fintendo!

And, for once in my life, I feel absolutely certain that nothing – and I mean NOTHING – can possibly go wrong.

Chapter 6

OH MY COD!

I've passed every exam I took with flying colours! Mrs Shelby pats me on the head as I re-read the results just to make sure. But it's true – I've come top in almost everything! I am thirty-three tail-flips and a shark-smile happy!

Mum and Dad are just as excited when I get home from school and tell them the good news. We swim happy circles around the kitchen and knock a pack of kelp krispies over. The krispies float through the water and start sticking to our skin. All three of us look like we've been covered in barnacles!

Then Dad shakes my fin. "Well done, son," he says, wiping a kelp krispie from his eye. "We're so proud of you."

"Yes we are!" says Mum, giving me a massive hug. "Well done, Starfish! Now you can really enjoy the end-of-term party tonight."

I get a sudden fluttery feeling in my tummy.

Now that I've passed my exams, it's time for me to bag that Fintendo!

The school sports hall has been decorated for the end-of-term party. Well, when I say decorated, what I mean is that a few strings of Christmas lights have been strung up, and a huge glitter-pearl is hanging from the ceiling. A couple of really bored-looking lantern fish are taking it in turns to shine on it.

"I don't think much of the music," Joe mutters.

Ralph and Tony nod in agreement.

The DJ (also known as Mrs Shelby) is playing some rubbish music from the olden days. They're songs my mum and dad like!

A table of nibbles is set up against the far wall. Two rows of chairs line the long walls on either side of the hall. One side has the boys sitting on them, the other has the girls. Both lines are staring at the other, but not saying a word.

Pearl and Cora are in their ballet skirts and doing some dance moves. They must be warming up for the contest.

"Are you sure you're going to be able to beat them?" Ralph whispers.

I nod and grin. I haven't told my mates about my street-dancing lessons down at the skate park. I want it to be a surprise.

Then I see Rick and Donny over by the food table. They're tapping their fins along to the music. Rick is all dressed up for the contest in his leather jacket and sunglasses. Yeah well, he might look cool now but seeing me dance will wipe that smirk off his face.

"Oh my cod! Look at that!" Ralph says, pointing a fin towards the dance

floor. Two ancient teachers – Mr Kelp and
Mrs Clambury – are dancing together.
Well, they're trying to dance together but
Mr Kelp slips, pulls a fin and has to be
helped back to his chair.

It's all majorly embarrassing.

But I'm not really bothered. I'm
here for one thing only, and that's the
dance contest. I look at the clock, and my
tummy churns with nerves. I turn round
to chat to Ralph, Joe and Tony, but they've
swum over to the nibbles table.

I'm just about to join them when
Mrs Shelby stops the music and speaks
into the microphone. "Okay, everyone, it's

time for the dance contest."

Pearl and Cora start squealing.

"The first round is a dance-off," Mrs Shelby continues. "Will all contestants please swim over to the dance floor. I want you to all start dancing and if I call your name it means you're out. I'll keep going until only three acts are left! There are no rules about what kind of dancing you do. This is your chance to freestyle!"

The music begins and I start going through the moves Lola and Shark Beatz have been teaching me over the last few weeks. I don't want to get a big hammer or anything, but I can tell everyone's kind of impressed.

"Where d'you learn to dance like that, Harry?" someone shouts.

"Awesome moves, Harry!" Tony calls. Joe waves his tentacles in time and starts glowing pink with excitement.

"Yeah, yeah, very cool," says Ralph, "but can you please hurry up so I can have something to eat!"

"Billy Bullshark, you're out!" Mrs Shelby calls through the microphone. "And Sarah Shellfish, I'm afraid you're not through to the next round."

I don't look at anyone else, I just keep focusing on my moves.

"Kevin Killerwhale, I'm afraid you're out too," Mrs Shelby calls. "Kevin, put your teeth away this minute! And come and see me after the competition. There's no need to be such a bad loser! Lacy Lungfish, nice try, but I'm sorry, you're out."

And so it goes on.

I keep on dancing – and hoping with every fin on my body that I won't hear Mrs

Shelby call my name. And then, suddenly, the music goes silent. I keep on dancing, too scared to stop.

"Harry Hammer!" Mrs Shelby calls and my heart sinks.

I'm out!

"Oh, man!" I sigh, swimming over to Ralph, Joe and Tony. I don't know why they're grinning. Some friends they are!

"Don't look so gloomy, Harry," Mrs Shelby says. "You're through to the final."

WHHHHAAAAAAAATTTTTTTT?!

I turn back round. Only the twins and Rick are left on the dance floor. Ralph, Joe and Tony start finning and tentacle-ing me on the back. I've done it! I'm through to the next round. It's me against Rick and Pearl and Cora!

"Congratulations, dancers!" Mrs Shelby cries. "Now it's time for our finalists to perform their individual routines. Pearl and Cora, you're first."

Pearl and Cora fluff up their skirts and start to dance. Although it's ballet, it's actually quite good. They twirl and kick and turn in perfect time to the music. As they finish, the crowd goes wild. The twins curtsey and wave as they swim off the dance floor.

"Next up, Rick Reef!" Mrs Shelby

cries. Rick swims
into the centre of
the dance floor and
starts doing the
coolest dive-jive I
have ever seen. The
light bouncing off
the glitter-pearl
sparkles on his blue-whale shoes and his
tail is a blur.

Rick finishes with a
fin-stand and awesome
dorsal flip.

It's so good, even
I'm clapping!

Then suddenly, I feel scared. If I'm not even cooler than Rick and even more graceful than the dolphin twins, that Fintendo is never going to be mine.

I take my Shark Beatz cap and shipwreck bling out of my pocket and put them on. I'm going to have to pull out all the stops.

And that means I'm going to have to do my signature move – the immense Hammerhead Spin!

The music booms out. I start busting every move that Lola and Shark Beatz have drilled into me.

"Go, Harry!" Ralph yells.

"Come on!" Joe and Tony shout, clapping their tentacles and fins in time.

I am a ship-hop king! Just like Moby the Eighth (but better at dancing and without all the headless wives). The light from the glitter-pearl starts bouncing off my bling and reflecting all around the room. I start Six-Tailing in circles across the floor. My cap is on backwards and my tracksuit is flapping. The music gets faster. I'm Plopping. I'm Docking. I Drop better than I ever have before. The crowd are clapping along. Whooping and yelling.

I am ON FIRE.

One last Treasure-Chest Pop into

111

the sickest Catfish Daddy and I'm upside down and ready! The Head Spin starts out well and the sports hall becomes a blur as I spin faster. But then something terrible happens...

1. My hammer twists the water around me like a ship's propeller...

2. In the skate park, this only twirled the spectators around with it...

3.   But in the closed space of the sports hall...
       IT'S A DISASTER!

4.   CRASH! ARRRRRRRRRRRGH! SPLAT!
       SMASH! OOOOOOOOOOHHHHH!
       BOING! FLUBBBERRRRRRRRRRRRR!!!
       KERRRRRRRRRRRRRRUNCH!!!!!!!!!!

By the time the room stops spinning,
everyone is covered in food. And the boy
fish are twisted up with the girl fish.

       Awkward.

       Mrs Shelby's glasses are upside
down and the rest of the teachers are
downside up. Pearl is somehow wearing
Rick's leather jacket, and Rick is floating

113

backwards trying to get his tail out of her pink skirt.

Joe and Tony are stuck to the ceiling, clinging to the glitter-pearl for dear life. Ralph is the only one who seems to be okay. He's been flung into the centre of a huge trifle and is now happily eating his way out of it.

But I'm right in the middle of the devastation – my hammer still vibrating from the worst self-induced flubber of all time.

Mrs Shelby staggers out from behind the DJ decks. The other teachers start helping everyone untangle

themselves from each other, and wipe
the food off their faces.

"HARRY!" Mrs Shelby yells in her
sternest voice. "HARRY!"

"Y-y-y-yes, Miss?"

"You are..." Mrs Shelby
pauses to put her glasses back
the right way up.

"Y-y-y-y-yes, Miss?"

"You are DISQUALIFIED!"

I hang my hammer in shame.

"Tonight's winners are Pearl and Cora," Mrs Shelby says.

Rick lets out a loud boo.

"And it is with great pleasure that I present you with this prize of a Fintendo SeaWii-DS!"

I'm all ready for this to be the worst moment of my life ever. But then I see the Fintendo. It's pink and glittery and TOTALLY GIRLY.

My Head Spin may have wrecked the sports hall, but it gave me the luckiest escape in gaming history. Rick would have made my life hell if I'd won THAT!

And anyway, I might not have a Fintendo but at least I've passed my exams and won't have to do any more revision for a very long time. I've got the whole summer holiday ahead of me to hang out with my best buddies. And I'll be able to see loads more of my new friends Lola and Shark Beatz. No, things aren't too bad at all!

When I get home, the house is very quiet. Mum and Dad must either be out at some boring event, or they've already gone to bed.

My bedroom door is open, but it's dark inside. "Larry, can I have some light, please," I call to my lantern fish as I swim inside. Nothing happens. I hope I don't have to change his bulb again – it's so fiddly and I always get covered in lantern-fish snot.

"**SURPRISE!!!!!!!!!!!!!!!!!!!!!!!!!!**"

I nearly jump out of my skin as the room is flooded with light. Mum and Dad are standing in the middle of the room, with Humphrey and Lenny. All of them have the biggest smiles on their faces.

"We wanted to give you a special surprise, Harry," Mum says. "To say well done for passing your exams and working so hard at your revision."

"Yes," says Dad, "we're very impressed with how seriously you've taken your studies."

Mum laughs. "And to think I was worried

that all you wanted to do was play on a Fintendo."

I pull my best serious face and shake my head.

"So, to say thank you for all your hard work..." Mum says, pulling a box out from behind her, "we've bought you this!"

When I see what's on the box I almost faint in shock. It's a Fintendo!

I can't believe it. I open the box with trembling fins. Instead of a pink, glittery, GIRLY Fintendo, there's a brilliant blue, awesomely shiny Fintendo – complete with loads of games!

AMAZING!!!!!!!!!!!!!!!!!!!!!!!!!!

I'm so happy I even hug Mum
and Dad without feeling embarrassed.
After they leave the room, I high-fin
Humphrey and Lenny.

"Still think your mum is an evil dictator, then, Harry?" laughs Humphrey.

But I don't have time to answer.

I'm too busy firing up Super Snapper Races 8!

Have you read...

these funny fishy tales
from Harry and the gang?

Shark School : Book 1
ISBN: 978-1-84877-732-3

Shark Star : Book 2
ISBN: 978-1-84877-733-0

Lone Shark : Book 3
ISBN: 978-1-84877-734-7

Shark Alert : Book 4
ISBN: 978-1-84877-735-4

www.harry-hammer.co.uk

STINKY and JINKS

My Hamster is a Genius
ISBN: 978-1-84877-293-9

My Hamster is an Astronaut
ISBN: 978-1-84877-294-6

My Hamster is a Spy
ISBN: 978-1-84877-295-3

My Hamster's Got Talent
ISBN: 978-1-84877-167-3

www.stinkyandjinks.blogspot.co.uk